Praise for
When Winnie Went Away

"There are bereavement storybooks for young children and… detailed books for grieving adults, but not many books for people in between. The imaginings in this book…fill the gap and soothe heartache in a way not previously written about."

KAREN SHAW BECKER, DVM

"An inspiring and charming story filled with healing and spiritual wisdom. I highly recommend this helpful book for anyone who is recovering from a loss."

TRUDY GRISWOLD, AUTHOR OF *ANGELSPEAKE*

"Gentle, simple, and compassionate…It is impossibly difficult to lose an animal companion. *When Winnie Went Away* is an invaluable resource for anyone who has ever loved and lost a pet."

PAT MILLER, CBCC-KA, CPDT-KA, PEACEABLE PAWS LLC

"This book presents a unique approach to the death of a pet (or anyone else)…a very valuable resource for all those who grieve deeply… which may very well be all of us."

DORY DZINSKI, LICENSED PROFESSIONAL COUNSELOR,
TRAUMA DEBRIEFER

"When Winnie Went Away is a beautifully crafted, multi-dimensional exploration of the concept of death to help children understand and process loss – and life! Kreitler delivers her healing messages uniquely and creatively, always reminding us that at the heart of everything is love."

LISA JACOBY, PROFESSIONAL DEVELOPMENT COACH/CONSULTANT

"This story guides the reader gently, lovingly, and imaginatively along a path that starts to heal the feelings of sorrow and loss that occur when a beloved pet dies….
A great book for children as well as adults!"

KATE KENNEDY, EqTPM, CST EQUINE MUSCLE THERAPIST

"…adorable and wise."

ROBIN QUINN, BOOK CONSULTANT

When Winnie Went Away

When Winnie Went Away

by
Bonnie Kreitler

Illustrations by Carole Ohl

RAMBLING DOG PUBLICATIONS LLC
Southport, Connecticut

When Winnie Went Away

Copyright © 2023 Bonnie Kreitler

Rambling Dog Publications LLC
Easton, CT 06612
www.ramblingdog.com

ISBN: 978-0-9970653-0-5 (Paperback Edition)
ISBN: 978-0-9970653-1-2 (eBook Edition)

Library of Congress Control Number: 2021908387
Full information available on WorldCat and SkyRiver

Dog Illustrations by Carole Ohl
Cover Design by 100 Covers
Interior Design by Integrative Ink

To three generations of muses–
Pet, Lou, and little Emma

Contents

All the world's a stage,
And all the men and women merely players;
They have their exits and their entrances,
And one man in his time plays many parts...

William Shakespeare
As You Like It, Act 2, Scene 7

Author's Note

This story offers possibilities to ease the hurt when a furry—or hooved, feathered, scaly, or slimy—best friend leaves your life.

Like a play, the story unfolds in dialogue alone as a series of conversations between two neighbors. Only dogs have names and genders. Details about the neighbors are left to the reader's imagination to fill in as it suits their own life experiences.

Use the conversations as prompts to imagine ways to deal with the pain of your own losses. Read the words to yourself. Or read the dialogue out loud to someone whose heart aches.

Whatever way you use this book, my wish is that this story softens grief's sharp edges and leaves its readers feeling just a little bit better.

Blessings on anyone who holds this book in their hands.

CHAPTER 1

Listening

Hi. My mom sent me over with this mail. It's yours, but we got it by mistake.

Did you hear? About the accident?

Mrs. Gordon called last night to tell me about it. I wasn't home over the weekend when it happened.

I heard that Winnie died. I'm so very sorry.

Thanks. I'm trying not to cry too much because it makes Mom sad again. Then she starts crying again. But it's hard. The house seems empty without him. I miss Winnie so much.

Well, it's certainly OK for kids or grown-ups to cry when they lose a pet. A best buddy. In fact, it's pretty normal. Would you like to sit here on the steps and tell me what happened?

Somebody left the gate open. Winnie ran into the street in front of a car. It hit him. I heard it hit him! He was just lying there. He didn't move. And the lady driving the car was screaming.

I started running out of the yard, but Mom grabbed me and wouldn't let me go out in the street to get him. I know I could have helped Winnie! Maybe I could have saved him! Dad went out and picked him up, and put him in the car. And I never saw Winnie again. He's just... gone. I really miss him a lot.

You loved Winnie. It always hurts to lose someone you love. I remember how excited you were when he came as a puppy. What made Winnie special to you? What do you miss about him most?

I miss how he was so wild and wiggly when I came home from school.

It is hard when your special buddy isn't there to greet you.

Yeah. And I miss his doggy kisses and his smelly doggy breath. I miss cuddling with him and using him as a pillow when we watched TV.

Did Winnie sleep with you?

He stayed in my room at night to keep me company. And sometimes, I snuck him into my bed. But Mom didn't like that. I always felt safe when Winnie was with me.

I feel that way about my Sammy too.

When I came home from school today, I just got so sad because he wasn't there. I feel just...alone. And I miss the way Winnie always loved me, even if I did something that wasn't nice. Winnie never yelled at me or gave me a time-out. No matter what!

Ahh. You have a lot of reasons to miss him. Dogs have a way of making us feel like the most important person in the world. They make us feel good about ourselves. It's hard to lose that kind of friend.

Yeah. I can't believe he's gone and I'll never see him again! Or snuggle with him again. I'm glad I came over. I feel a little better talking about Winnie. Did you ever have a dog that died?

Oh, I've known and lost quite a few dogs. And other animals, too. I grew up on a farm, and I saw many animals born and many die. There's a cycle of coming and going to life. Like how plants pop out of the ground when it warms up come spring, grow into flowers come summer, then scatter a bunch of seeds in fall. After those tiny seeds hibernate in the ground all winter, a new plant comes again in spring. Comings and goings. Comings and goings.

Winnie died suddenly. And that makes it harder. But the truth is, all dogs have shorter lives than people. Even the dogs that do grow old, for a dog. I know my Sammy will probably die before I do. But that doesn't keep me from being happy about having her with me now.

Myself, I don't like the feel of the words "die" or "dead." They don't seem to describe all the comings and goings of the animals in my life just right.

What do you mean?

Well, "die" and "dead" seem to say that everything about an animal is just "gone" when it stops breathing. Nothing is left. As if a dog or a cat was just a bag of skin and bones. That never seemed to be the whole story to me, especially when I was your age. I thought about it pretty hard when I lost my first dog, Buster. Grown-ups said things that just didn't make sense to me.

And then, a very kind neighbor, Miss Elaine, showed me a way to see things a bit differently. She helped me imagine Buster in a story that made me feel a little better. Over the years, I've remembered that story. Even imagined it working out in different ways. I've added my own bit to the story, come to think of it.

What is it? Can you tell me the story?

Hmmm. I don't tell the story to everyone. And I'm really careful about telling it to some people.

Why?

Well, a lot of people, particularly grown-ups, have pretty set ideas about what "die" and "dead" mean. And if your ideas and their ideas aren't the same, they get upset.

Set and upset. That's funny! Why do they get upset by a story?

I'm not exactly sure why. But, to understand the story, you need to imagine. And some grown-ups can't use their imaginations the way they could when they were a kid like you. If you can't imagine, it's hard to see things any other way than the way you already see them. So, people hang on to believing whatever they believe about dogs or people being dead, even if it keeps them stuck in being miserable and sad.

Won't you be sad when Sammy dies?

Oh, I'll really miss Sammy when she goes. Just like you miss Winnie now. Only I don't think of "dead" as "gone forever" anymore. I'll be sad for a while. That's just normal. But I won't stay stuck in being sad forever.

Miss Elaine's story helped me imagine that there was a part of Buster that was still around. And she showed me a way to connect with that part. Feeling I could still connect somehow with Buster made me a little less sad.

You mean like a ghost?

No, not a ghost. More like… an imaginary friend. Or like the stuffed animals you used to play with and talk to. And they talked back to you. And together, you made up little stories that you acted out and had fun with.

What was the story she told you? Can you tell me?

I wonder. Are you too old to understand?

That's a funny thing to say! My mom sometimes tells me I'm too young to understand some things. So how can I be too old to understand?

To understand the story, you have to use your imagination. Can you still imagine? Can you imagine that maybe, just maybe, Winnie had an invisible "love spark," something that made him a special dog, a particular dog, not just any old dog?

You mean like a soul?

Well, you could call it that if you like. But there we go again. Soul, spirit, ghost! Those words mean different things to different people. So, the way you use those words can agitate some people.

What do you mean?

I mean that if someone doesn't agree with you about exactly what those words mean, they get all bothered. They want to argue about the words instead of listening to the story. Soul, spirit, ghost! I'm careful with those words. They mean so many different things to different people.

I only know that it seems to me that there's some kind of "spark"—something like the electricity that runs through wires inside the walls in our houses and lights up light bulbs—that seems to make the difference between being alive and being dead. We can't see it, but we can tell when it's there and when it's not.

When the spark was there, Winnie could run and jump, bark and wag, and give kisses and all that stuff. And the spark was gone when Winnie's heart stopped beating and his lungs stopped pumping. Kind of like flipping a light switch off. His body didn't move anymore. Or maybe it's the other way around. First, the spark goes away, and then the heart and all that stuff stops working. I'm not sure. It doesn't matter.

Either way, Winnie's body wasn't moving anymore when the car flipped his switch, and his spark left. Something that was there before, something that made him alive, was gone.

That spark gave him his own personality, things that made him different from other dogs. But something even more than that. Something that animated him and made him different from say, a rock.

You mean like the way he always followed me everywhere when I was home?

And how he wagged his tail so hard it hurt when he hit me with it?

And the way he was crazy for chasing balls and swimming?

And ice cream! He loved ice cream so much that he snatched a whole cone out of my hand! Boy, was I mad!

Yes, like that. And can you imagine that his spark didn't stop being Winnie just because his body stopped moving? Can you imagine what Winnie's spark might be doing if it was still around, even though you can't see it, or feel it, or hear it?

I think so. I want to. I could try!

Well, then maybe you are young enough to hear the story.

CHAPTER 2

All the World a Stage

Over time, I've come to call the story "The Big Play."

But before I tell you how *I imagine* the Big Play, I'll tell you the story about how I heard of it in the first place.

I grew up on a farm. My grandpa lived on the farm with us. When I was a bit younger than you, he died. He was pretty old, and one day, he got pretty sick. After that, he stayed in bed all the time. My mother took care of him. Then I came home from a friend's house one day, and Grandpa was gone. He'd just left. He never said anything to me about where he was going. Or when he was coming back.

My mother said he wasn't coming back. She said things I didn't understand, like, "It was expected," or, "It was his time to go." Gradually,

I understood that I would never get to ride on the tractor with him again. Or go fishing. Or go into town with him to get ice cream and library books. He used to say we were tight! We were buddies.

A lot of grown-ups came to the house. They said more things I couldn't understand. Like, "He passed," or "He's gone to his reward," or "He's with the angels." None of what they said helped me figure out where he had gone at all. One old guy said, "He bought the farm," and smiled and seemed to think that was a good thing to say.

Why could it be good if your grandpa died?

Well, it was just something people back then used to say when someone died, and they didn't know what else to say. But, just like you, it made no sense to me that saying some things made them sad and saying other things made them smile. None of the things they said made me feel any better at all. They just reminded me that Grandpa was gone. I'd never sit on his lap again or get a quarter that he'd pulled from behind my ear.

I did figure out that it was OK to be sad. And even though the grown-ups were sad, they threw a party for my grandpa. My mother said the party was for him, even though he wasn't there. I knew he would have liked the cake. But I wished he'd walk into the room and be with us.

I wish Winnie would walk up to us right now.

It's a big ache, isn't it? I understand how it feels because our dog Buster died not very long after that. He was old, too, like my grandpa. But when Buster died, no one came to the house for a party. When

I was sad about him, people would say, "You'll get another dog," or, "You'll get over him in time," or, "He was just a dog." Everybody acted as though not much had happened. It wasn't as OK to be sad or cry. And that just made me sadder.

My aunt said some things like that. It kind of made me mad.

People often mean well. They're just trying to say something to cheer you up, even if it doesn't. One lady, though, helped me make some sense of it all. That was Miss Elaine. She lived down the road from us, and she came to the farm every week to buy eggs from my mother.

She came along one day shortly after Buster died. I was sitting on the porch steps feeling sad about Buster, and about my grandpa, and about how both my best buddies weren't around anymore. She sat on the steps with me for a bit, not saying anything right away. She seemed to know Buster and Grandpa were on my mind.

Then she quietly told me that it helped her think of life as a Big Play whenever a good friend died. All the people in the world—and animals like Winnie—are, like, actors in the play, she said. The actors all take turns going on stage, adding their bit to the play's story, then they go offstage behind the curtains again.

So, she said, my grandpa and Buster were still nearby, just backstage. They weren't *gone* forever, just out of sight. And she told me if I clapped my hands really hard and told them how much I loved how they'd played their parts in the Big Play while they were on stage, they would hear me clapping. And they would feel my love through all my hurt.

I liked the idea of Buster and Grandpa being nearby, just behind a curtain, where they could still see and hear me even if I couldn't see or hear them. So, I tried clapping my hands a little. It did cheer me up a bit. To feel there was some way to tell them how much I still loved them.

Then Miss Elaine started clapping with me. Then we began clapping harder and harder and louder and louder! We made so much noise! Then we started laughing. My mother came out of the house to see what in the world was going on. When Miss Elaine went inside to get her eggs, I sat on the porch feeling a little bit better than I had before.

Since then, I've thought about the Big Play a lot, especially when something happens and I don't understand why. It helps me think things through a bit. It gives me a little bit of a different way of seeing things.

Could we clap for Winnie?

Sure! Let's see who can clap louder!

CHAPTER 3

Imagining

Thanks for clapping with me. That does make me feel a little better about Winnie. He was my best, most special friend. And did you hear me whistle? I just learned to whistle. And when I whistled, Winnie would come running SO fast!

I like thinking about Winnie just being backstage where he can hear me clapping for him. But who makes up the Big Play? Why couldn't they make it up so Winnie didn't have to die?

Ah, well, as I imagine it, the Big Play is kind of messy compared to most plays.

Messy! Why?

Well, for one thing, most plays have just a few actors. But everyone in the whole world is in the Big Play. Together. All at the same time.

So EVERYBODY EVERYWHERE in the whole world is in the play?

That's how I imagine it.

Wow, that many people would need a humongous stage!

We have one! The whole Earth is the stage for the Big Play.

So, dogs are actors too? And all the other animals? And birds?
Yup!

What about plants?

Well, a play needs some scenery, right?

So the grass, and the trees, and the rain, and the sky, are all scenery in the play?

Everything! All the rocks, and rivers, and oceans, and mountains, and houses, and cars. Everything we see is all part of the scenery in the Big Play.

Even Winnie's toys?

Yup.

Who makes up the play?

Well, the way I imagine it, we all do. Together.

We do? What do you mean?

Well, no one person writes the whole script. We all make the story up together as we go along. We improvise.

What's a script? And what does improvise mean?

Well, in a usual play, someone writes out exactly all the things that all the actors are supposed to say. They describe where the actors should stand, how they should wave their arms, how they should stomp around, and all that. That's a script.

The things the actors say are called their lines. The actors memorize their lines. That means they know them by heart and can say them without a script to read from. Then they practice saying their lines together. That's called a rehearsal. One person, the director, tells them when to come out from behind the curtain onto the stage. And the director tells them when to go backstage behind the curtain again.

The director tells the actors just how to say their lines. Like, should they whisper their lines, or should they shout them? Should they sound happy or sad or mad when they say them? And the director tells the actors where they should stand on the stage and whether they should wave or stomp or stand still or whatever else it might say in the script.

Meanwhile, the director tells another bunch of people what kind of scenery to build. Different parts of the play happen in different places. So, they build scenery for each of those different places. Finally, the actors dress up in costumes that make them look like the characters in the play.

Everything about the play is decided before the actors go onstage. They practice saying the lines and moving around. At last, the actors are ready. They go on stage and speak the lines the writer wrote. They wave and stomp around the way the director directed them. Different actors come and go during the play, on and off the stage, when it's their turn. And at the end, ALL the actors come out from behind the curtain and bow to the audience. And the audience claps to let the actors know how much they liked the play and how the actors acted it out.

The Big Play is a lot messier. And much more fun, I think. For one thing, there are way more animals like dogs in it. In the Big Play, the actors decide what part they want to play. Nobody tells them what to say or what to do. They just go on the stage, see what's already going on, and jump right in. They may have ideas about what they want to do in the play. But they don't figure out how they're going to wave or stomp or sing or dance until they get on stage. They all just make it up as they go along. That's called improvising.

That's crazy! What if everybody tries to talk at the same time? Or run around at the same time? They'd be bumping into each other! And tripping over the dogs! It sounds like a mess!

Messy, yes! Sometimes it is! But a lot more interesting than just following somebody's script. Think about your own day. You don't know exactly everything you're going to say or do when you get out of bed in the morning, do you?

Well, sort of. I know I'm going to go to school and stuff.

True enough. We all have routines, things we do pretty much the same way every day. And those are a bit like scripts. But what would happen if the school bus didn't come one morning because the driver got sick and they couldn't find a substitute in time?

I guess my mom or dad would have to take me to school.

There it is! That's you and your mom and dad improvising together. And what if you got to school and, because you were late, you hustled to get inside? And because you were hurrying, you tripped and fell. And when you fell, you cut your hand or your knee. Now, what do you do?

I guess I'd go to the nurse's office to get the cut cleaned and get a bandage. Then I'd be REALLY late for class, and I'd have to explain why to the teacher. And my teacher would probably ask someone in my class to help me catch up with whatever they were doing. Improvising, right?

Right. You and the nurse, and the teacher, and your classmates would all improvise together when a routine falls apart. Welcome to the Big Play!

The thing about having such a really Big Play, with so many actors, is that no one actor controls the whole play. And there's no director. The story could go this way or that way depending on what each actor thinks or does or how whole bunches of actors act out at the time.

So, I can't say why Winnie died just now. Only that he did. Sometimes, down the road, we might come to understand that whatever happened, happened for a reason. So that something else could happen. Sometimes not. Maybe we'll figure it out when it's our turn to go back behind the stage curtain. I'd like to imagine that.

But when things that make me sad happen, I try to look for a different perspective, a different angle to see it from, a different way to look at the situation. One that helps me feel a little better about it.

What do you mean?

Imagine, for instance, that when it was time for Winnie to get ready to go on stage, Winnie decided to be a certain kind of dog with a certain personality. Say he wanted to be a friendly dog who loved swimming and eating ice cream. And then he picked out a costume that suited that personality. Say a black dog with webbed paddle paws for fast swimming.

And Winnie might have decided that he would like to be in a family with children he could play with. And that the children lived in a town with places to swim. And maybe he even peeked from behind the curtain, saw *your* family on stage, and thought, "Wow! I want to be *that* family's dog!" Then he got ready, waited for his cue to go on stage, and jumped out to join you.

Do you think Winnie picked our family out? That he picked me out to be a best friend?

I like to imagine that's possible.

So, he loved me even before he became Winnie?

I think that's possible too.

Now I love Winnie more than ever. I'd still like to cuddle with him one more time. But I do feel a little better. Can we clap for Winnie again?

Sure! Ready? Set? GO!

CHAPTER 4

What If

Hi, little neighbor! What's up at your house this afternoon?

My mom said to thank you for the pot of flowers you brought over yesterday. She said they cheered her up.
I'm glad. How about you? How are *you* feeling today?

Well, I liked the Big Play story you told me yesterday. It made me feel a little better about losing Winnie. I told my mom about it. But I still miss Winnie an awful lot. It was hard at school today to pretend everything was OK. My teacher kept telling me to pay attention.

But I'm really mad at my sister.

How come?

I think she left the gate open. She was the last one in the yard after we came home from soccer practice.

Did you see her leave it open?

No. But she was the last one in. How could she be so stupid? It was all her fault!

Hmmm. Could it have happened any other way?

Well, maybe. The mailman came by with a package for Mom. Maybe he left the gate open.

Sounds like that's a possibility too.

And one time, Winnie got so excited when another dog was walking across the street. He scratched so hard at the gate that the latch jiggled open. He was such a silly!

There you go. There's more than one possibility for why the gate was open.

So maybe it wasn't all my fault?

Ahh, why do you say that?

Mom said I was supposed to watch our little sister while we played in the yard.

I see. Well, it sounds to me like some improvising was going on.

Like the Big Play?

Exactly. So many actors, all moving around doing their own thing. You, your sister, Winnie, the mailman, your mother, and the lady driving the car. What if the lady had taken a different street? What if I had been walking by, saw the gate open, and closed it? What if Winnie had gone down the sidewalk instead of running into the street? No one can say exactly precisely who caused what.

All we know for sure is that a bunch of actors was involved. And when all the improvising came together, you lost Winnie. That's what I meant about how the Big Play can get messy.

Yeah. I hadn't thought about what happened to Winnie as improvising.

But I'm still mad. I'm mad at my mom. She took all of Winnie's stuff—his bed and his bowls and his toys—and everything is just gone. Just like Winnie. And not seeing them anymore makes me miss Winnie even more.

Maybe your mom misses Winnie too. Maybe she hid his dishes and toys because seeing them made her sad. Did you ask her why she picked them up?

No. I'm still mad at her. And I'm especially mad at my dad.

Seems like you're angry about a lot of things. Why are you mad at your dad?

He took Winnie to the vet and never brought him home. I should have made sure the gate was closed. I loved Winnie. I would never hurt him.

But when my dad came home without him, I knew it was my fault. I never got to see Winnie again!

Well, your dad was improvising along with everyone else when the accident happened.

What if he had brought Winnie home? Would it have made you feel better to see Winnie again? Even if he wasn't breathing? He wasn't moving? Or would that have made you feel even sadder?

I'm not sure. I only know I'm mad! It's not fair! Why couldn't the improvising go so that Winnie was still here?

Imagine what might have happened if Winnie hadn't run out of the yard.

Then he would still be here!

Maybe. But you told me that the gate was open. And your little sister was in the yard with you.

Yeah.

Well, imagine Winnie saw your little sister running toward the gate. And that excited Winnie and made him want to run, too. You know how he *loved* to run. So, he ran past your little sister and out the gate. But he was *so* excited that he forgot to look both ways and he ran into the street in front of the car. Maybe Winnie's running out ahead of her saved your sister from harm.

So you think Winnie was a hero?

Maybe. I can imagine Winnie being heroic. I remember how he was, always barking at strangers and protecting you kids.

Yeah, he was like that. I never thought about my sister running into the street and getting hurt.

Or here's another crazy idea. Let's say Winnie saw the car coming down the street. Maybe he decided he could show everyone how brave and fast he could be. He saw the gate open. He decided he would chase that car right off our street. Except that he made a mistake and forgot the part about how much bigger and faster cars are than dogs.

So, Winnie was improvising?

Maybe. It's hard to keep track of just what all the actors are up to all the time in the Big Play. Much less knowing why they're up to whatever they're doing. Maybe, for some reason we haven't thought of, it was just his time to go backstage again. Can you imagine the story in different ways?

I don't know. But I like making up stories about Winnie. And it makes me feel a little better to think Winnie was a hero.

Me too.

CHAPTER 5

Keeping the Sparks Alive

Hi. What are you doing?

Well, I'm tending my dog garden.

Dog garden! That sounds funny! Why do you call it a dog garden? Is it only for dogs?

I guess you could say that. See this little tree? It's a dogwood tree. And see those spotty leaves under the tree? Those are called dogtooth violets. They have pretty yellow flower bells every spring. That shrubby bush with tiny, white flowers by the fence is called dog fennel. And these pretty flowers I'm planting right now are called dog flowers.

Those are just like the flowers you gave Mom yesterday. Why do they call them dog flowers?

Well, you take one of the blossoms and hold it just so, then squeeze it just so, and it looks like a tiny dog barking.

Can I try it?

Sure. Pick one.

Arf, arf! That's funny!

Most people around here call them snapdragons. Mrs. Chopra told me that in India, where she grew up, the children called them dog flowers because you could make them look like they were barking. I liked that. So I decided to plant some in my dog garden.

A flower that barks! Can I take some home to show this to my sister?

Sure! Take as many as you like.

So you call it a dog garden because all the plants have dog names?

That, and also because we buried two of our dogs here.

You mean it's a dog cemetery?

Just for our dogs. One was very small. She was a feisty little terrier named Toby.

Toby! That's a boy's name.

Well, in her case, it was a girl's name. Our kids named her after a character in a book they liked. So that was that.

Toby loved to snuggle on a particular blanket. So, we wrapped her little body up nice and snuggly in her blanket, tucked her into a nice box with her favorite toys, and now she's buried here. And we had a little celebration of her life. We clapped for her and told her what a great dog she'd been. The first dog we put in the dog garden was a *much* bigger dog named Roger.

Was Roger a boy?

Yes, he was a boy.

Then his name matched him.

Right. We found this dogwood when it was just a skinny little stick out in the woods on my brother's farm. We dug it up and put it in the ground here. But before we planted the dogwood, we scattered Roger's ashes in the bottom of the hole. Then we had a little celebration for him.

Roger's ashes? What do you mean?

Well, because Roger was so big, the veterinarian cremated him. That means they use very high heat to dry out the dog's body 'til it crumbles into a small pile of ashes. The ashes make it easier to bury the dog. Takes up less space. Some people keep the ashes someplace special in their house in a special box. Or they scatter them in a place that was special to their dog.

Does cremation hurt?

No, not at all. Remember how we talked about Winnie's love spark? Once the spark flies off, the dog's body doesn't feel anything anymore. So, cremation doesn't hurt.

By the way, I'm glad you stopped by. I found something I want to show you. It's up on the porch. Let's go look at it.

What is it?

It's my dog album. I've saved pictures of all the dogs I've had through the years.

Let me see! Are there pictures of Toby and Roger?

Yes, there are. Let's sit down here first. My knees could use a break from gardening. Then I can lay this album on the table so we can open it up.

Let's see. Toby and Roger are in this album somewhere. Here they are! Here and…here.

Wait. Turn that page back again. What's this dog's name?

That's Buster, the dog we had when I was small. When I first heard about the Big Play.

Is that you in the picture?

Yes, it is.

Buster was cute. But I can't believe you were ever that little! What are these?

Those are letters to Toby. She died when my children were just a bit older than you are. They were sad, just like you, when they lost their dog. So, we sat down and remembered all the things we loved about her, all the silly things she liked to do, her favorite things to eat, and stuff like that.

We wrote letters to her, like writing down her life story. Then we put them here in the album.

I like the pictures they drew of her in their letters. Look at all her spots! And that ball looks just like the tennis balls Winnie loved to chase and chew up.

Toby did love to chase balls, just like Winnie. And then she'd bury them. She was always digging. Especially in my flower garden!

You make me laugh.

Well, that's a good sign.

A sign of what?

A sign that you're feeling a little better. And a sign that maybe you're ready to think about playing with Winnie again.

Playing with Winnie again? How?

Remember when I told you that you couldn't understand the Big Play unless you could imagine things? Well, you can imagine that you and Winnie are still buddies. That's why I like this album. I can look at it and remember the fun times with my dogs. And sometimes, I close my eyes and go play with them again.

Close your eyes and play?

Closing my eyes sometimes helps me imagine. Would you like me to show you how I bring my dogs back into my life again for a little while?

That sounds neat. Is it hard?

Not at all. Remember when you first moved next door, and you wanted a dog so badly? You talked and talked to me about getting a dog. You told me what color fur it would have, how big it would be, and what kind of ears it would have. You had quite the shopping list!

Seeing Winnie again just takes a bit of that same imagination you used to bring Winnie into your life in the first place.

So you just close your eyes? Like you're going to sleep?

Well, I guess I do get quiet and maybe a bit dreamy. But I don't go to sleep like a nap.

Can we play with Winnie right now?

Sure, we can. Let's get comfy here in our chairs, close our eyes, and relax a bit.

Take a few nice, slow breaths in and out, in and out, quietly in and out.

Keep your eyelids closed. Then relax your eyes. That's it. Now let your soft eyes drift up ever so slowly, ever so gently. Just as though you were looking up into the leaves of the little dogwood tree.

As you breathe softly in and out, feel yourself becoming very relaxed, very quiet. Quiet enough to hear whispers from behind the stage curtains.

And the soft feeling behind our eyes moves down and settles in our hearts. And our hearts open up like the petals of a beautiful flower. And behind our eyelids, in our imaginations, we notice that we're sitting in your house. Right near the door.

Now, from our open hearts, we softly call Winnie.

In your imagination, you hear a whine at the door. You go over to investigate. You open the door.
Winnie is sitting there. He starts wiggling around. His tail is wagging and wagging. He's panting and whining. He's so excited to see you!

And you're so excited to see him. You pet him and pet him, and hug him and hug him. You look into his big, brown eyes, and he wags his tail.

You realize he wants you to take him for a walk. And you're so ready to take him. You open the door and go outside. The two of you go out the gate and down the street to the park.

Winnie brought a ball! He runs ahead of you, teasing you with the ball. You run after him, so happy to be playing with him again.

You play so hard that you both flop down on the ground. Winne rests his chin on your chest. You pet Winnie. You're so glad to be with him again.

A breeze picks up and reminds you it's time to go home. You and Winnie walk home, so happy to be together. You get to the gate and open it. But Winnie sits on the sidewalk outside. His tail wags with the promise to come back to play again whenever you call him. But, right now, he has to go back behind the curtain.

You stroke his soft head. You promise to call him back to play again soon. He picks up his ball and trots away. You turn and come back into the house. You sit and close your eyes again, enjoying the warm feeling of the love you and Winnie shared a little longer.

Now, slowly, open your eyes. And take a deep breath. And another.

What did you see?

It was awesome imagining being with Winnie again! I thought it would make me sad, but it didn't. I really could feel Winnie's love! Do you think he felt mine?

Oh, yes.

That's kind of like imagining a play, isn't it? We just made up a play about Winnie and me, didn't we?

Yes, we did. You can use your imagination to play with Winnie again, wherever you want, whenever you want. Just talk to Winnie. Just play with him. Tell him anything. Tell him how you feel because you can't still feel and smell and hug him. Then go ahead and imagine you're doing those things anyway.

Even though Winnie's furry self isn't with you, his love spark *is*. You can connect with him in whatever way feels good to you. If you want, you can hold a picture of Winnie or a stuffed dog that reminds you of him.

Do you think Winnie saw the play we imagined?

More than that. His love spark was right here on stage with you, improvising and loving every minute of it. And right now, I can imagine he'd like to connect with some of the cake I made this afternoon. Let me get some for us—and some lemonade to go with it?—while you look at that album some more.

CHAPTER 6

Possibilities

Welcome home, little neighbor. I was just finishing up my gardening when I saw your bus pull up. Lots of homework tonight? That backpack is bulging with books! And it looks like my mailbox is bulging with catalogs! Is that a new friend I saw you waving at when you got off the bus?

Yeah, I have a lot to read. That girl just moved here, and she's in my class. We both like our teachers. And we both like dogs!

I told her about Winnie. And she said that dogs go over a Rainbow Bridge to a giant playground when they die. They get to stay there and play there with lots of other dogs and animals. Then when we die, we get to cross the Rainbow Bridge. And when we get to the other side, our dogs come running to greet us. We get to be together again. Is that true?

Who knows for sure? I've heard of the Rainbow Bridge, though. I can certainly imagine what it looks like. It certainly feels good to imagine that we'll see our pets again.

But if my animal friends all come running at once, I'm in trouble!

Why?

In my life, I've been with a whole lot of dogs and other animals, like cows and horses and chickens. If they all meet me at the Rainbow Bridge at the same time, they'll knock me over with their running and jumping and flapping and licking and prancing!

That would be messy! Like the Big Play, huh! Is the Rainbow Bridge like heaven?

Who knows? There are so many ideas about heaven! That's another one of those words that upset some grown-ups. If your idea about heaven is different from what they think about it, then they want to argue with you. Some people don't think there's a heaven place at all.

Then other people believe they died, went to heaven, and came back here again! But each of them tells a little bit different story about what it was like there. So heaven knows exactly what heaven is like!

What happens when dogs go backstage in the Big Play? Is that like heaven?

Well, I suppose you could think of it that way. That when an actor goes off stage behind the curtains, and you can't see them anymore, they've gone to heaven. What do you imagine that would be like?

I'd like to imagine Winnie would come back out on the stage and be with me again.

Let's imagine that Winnie was backstage for a long, long time. Ten years! Maybe more. Then, one day, you are walking along minding your own business, and suddenly, there he is! Standing right in front of you again! What would you do?

I'd be so happy!

Or you'd be so freaked out, you'd scream. Aaah! A ghost! Oh no! What do I do?

No, I wouldn't. Well, maybe. I'd be pretty surprised. Maybe I wouldn't believe it.

Right. But here's something different to imagine. What if Winnie went backstage for a while and then decided to go back on stage as a different character wearing a different costume? And what if Winnie's love spark was not just one spark but a ball of sparks? And the ball burst and scattered tiny sparks all over. And each little spark grabbed a different costume and bounced out onto the stage.

Now imagine you come across a whole litter of bouncy, squirmy puppies. And you look at them, and one gives you a particular feeling, a feeling like the feeling you had with Winnie. And the puppy acts just a little bit like Winnie used to act. And you say to yourself, "I feel like I know that dog."

Could that happen?

Well, things in nature do seem to happen in cycles that go around and around. The sun comes up once a day and goes down once a day. Every day. The tides down by the ocean come up and go down twice a day. Individual things might change a bit this way or that, but the general cycle of things keeps repeating the same way, over and over.

Take the flowers here in my dog garden. Especially that dog fennel! I cut the dead stalks back to the ground when it goes to sleep in the winter. It looks like it's gone. But come spring, new stalks grow up! They get covered with those pretty little flowers again. Then the flowers produce seeds. When the flowers fall off the stalks, those seeds get scattered all over the garden. When the stalks die back again, I cut them to the ground again.

Every year, the dog fennel and I go through the same cycle. Every spring, the dog fennel grows back a little bit the same but a little bit different too.

So I can imagine that as things come and go, and go around and around, someday you might find a dog that reminds you a lot of Winnie, even if that dog isn't just like him.

Can I tell you something weird? Last night, I thought I heard Winnie's collar tags jingling when I climbed into bed.

I told my sister, and she said I was crazy. She said I was just making it up. And my mom said it was just my imagination. But I'm SURE I heard them.

Well, you know I believe in imagination. I see the Rainbow Bridge and the Big Play and our memories of our pets as imaginary bridges that keep us connected to them. They help us keep them in our hearts and our minds. And bridges work both ways.

What do you mean?

Have you ever been to a school play when someone forgets where they're supposed to be standing? Or—even worse—forgets what they're supposed to say? And then, from behind the curtain, the teacher helps them out? She whispers the lines they're supposed to say just loud enough for them to hear her, but not loud enough for anybody in the audience to hear.

I've heard many people say they thought they heard their dog or smelled their dog. Or they even say they saw their dog out of the corner of their eye. Just a quick flash of fur. Just like you heard tags jingling.

I like to imagine those are little stage whispers from dogs, letting their people know they're still nearby, just behind the curtains. Reminding their people that they still love them. So you can tell your sister that I don't think you're crazy.

Speaking about gardens and cycles, would you like a little dogwood tree to remind you of Winnie? I have some potted up in the back-yard. I grew them from seeds from that dogwood tree right here in my garden. They're ready to put in the ground now.

Ask your mom. Come back and get one if she says yes.

That sounds great! I'm going to ask her right now!

CHAPTER 7

Planting Seeds

Thanks for the dogwood tree. And guess what? Guess! You're never going to guess what we did with it!

I can't imagine! You're so excited. It must be something important. Tell me!

Well, I told my mom about the dog album. And the Rainbow Bridge and the Big Play. And clapping and everything. And I told her how sad I was that I didn't get to say goodbye to Winnie and how all his stuff just went away. And GUESS WHAT?

I'm going to pop if you don't tell me!

Mom didn't throw away all Winnie's stuff! She just put it away for a while because, just like you said, it made her sad to see it around the house.

And THEN, my dad came home with a box from the vet. He said it had Winnie's ashes in it. So they didn't just leave Winnie at the vet and throw him away. I was so glad!

And THEN you know what happened?!

I'm listening.

We had a party for Winnie! My sister and I drew pictures. I drew a picture of Winnie. My sister drew a whole page full of bones for him. He loved bones. And we had cookies. And ice cream.

And then we made a dog garden for him!

My mom put Winnie's leash and a couple of his old toys into a nice box. Dad dug a hole in the corner of the yard next to the fence. We poured Winnie's ashes into the bottom. Then we put the box of toys in. Then we put the dogwood tree on top of that.

My sister helped me shove the dirt back into the hole. Dad stamped the dirt down with his foot and pounded a big stake in the ground next to the tree. Then he tied the tree to the stake so it would grow straight. Mom said it looks tall and proud.

Mom planted the dog flowers you gave us, and then she dumped a bag of mulch around, just like in your garden. So we have a dog garden now too! I like the idea of Winnie being in our yard again.

And I imagine he likes being there too. Did you hear Winnie's tags jingling again?

What? Do you think Winnie was there?

I can imagine him just behind the stage curtains, peeking out and watching how everyone in your family showed how much they loved him. I'm sure it made him feel very happy to know you haven't forgotten him. You still have a love connection. And he can stay alive in your imagination forever.

We clapped for him! Maybe he heard us. But he's not really alive anymore, is he?

Well, not in the sense that you need to feed him, give him water, and take him for walks anymore. But I imagine his little love spark is very much alive in your life. And you can bring it back any time you remember him in your heart. In your imagination, you can still hug him and play with him.

Like we did the other day?

Right. Like that.

Could we do that again?

Certainly. Last time we imagined Winnie was playing with you at the park. Where would you like to meet him today?

In his dog garden! In my yard, where we planted the tree for him. Just in case he wasn't watching. I want to tell him all about it. And how even though I'm not as sad as I was before, I still miss him. And I won't forget him. Ever.

OK. Let's sit out on the porch again. Get yourself settled, and we'll send Winnie some imaginary pictures of everything your family did for him. Do you remember how we started before?

Yes! Sit still, close your eyes, take some breaths, and look up inside your eyelids. Keep your eyes closed.

That's wonderful! You're a good listener, and you have a good memory!

So just like you remembered, we'll sit still and get comfy.

Let's close our eyes. And relax our eyes. We take a few nice, slow breaths. In and out, in and out, in and out. Hmmmmm. Now our eyes look up, ever so softly, ever so gently, behind our eyelids.

And we can see behind our eyelids, in our mind's eye, that we're in your yard. We're sitting right in front of the little dogwood tree in your new dog garden.

And the soft feeling moves down and settles around our hearts. And our hearts open up like beautiful dogwood flowers in spring. Now, from our hearts, we softly call Winnie.

We ask Winnie to join us in your yard to see his new garden.

Can you see Winnie coming from behind the curtain? He's so happy that you haven't forgotten him. He's so glad that you called him to play again.

You show him the new dog garden. "That's for you," you tell him. "We planted a dogwood tree, so we'll never forget you."

Tell Winnie about all the things you planted with the dogwood tree to remember him. His ashes. His collar. Some pictures you drew of him. And the little heart-shaped rock you found. Show him some mind pictures of you and your family planting all these things in his dog garden.

Tell Winnie you'll remember him every time you see the little tree. Tell him that he can come back and play in the yard and see the tree whenever he wants. You play with Winnie for a while. You hug him.

Remind him that you'll never forget him. You tell him you love him. Now let Winnie go backstage again. You say thank you. You say goodbye until the next time.

Sit and enjoy the warm feeling in your heart as long as you like. You can call Winnie again, another time, anytime you want. Then open your eyes whenever you're ready.

Thanks. I like doing that again. It makes me feel better about Winnie. I still miss him, but he doesn't feel as "gone" as before. I think he liked it too.

I can certainly imagine that he did.

CHAPTER 8

Say What?

Hi. What are you doing in your dog garden?

I'm looking for a glove I lost. I was using my gardening gloves yesterday. Now one of them is missing. I have a hunch it's somewhere over here. Want to help?

Sure. But what's a hunch?

It's a sort of suggestion or feeling, an idea that seems to come out of nowhere about something. Sometimes it's like being nagged. The same notion keeps popping into your head over and over again.

And I have a nagging feeling that my glove is somewhere over here, even though I don't remember working around here yesterday.

How do you get a hunch?

Oh, they just seem to come to people. It's an idea that just pops into your head. But, sometimes I ask Toby to help me find things. Then when an idea, a hunch, pops into my head, I pay attention to it.

Do you mean your dog Toby, the one you told me about? Isn't she buried here in the dog garden?

Yes, she is. That's the rock we used to mark where we buried her.

How can you ask her to help you find things?

Oh, it's a game we played when she was alive. So I imagine I'm playing it with her again, and it keeps me from getting all upset about whatever I lost until I find it again.

Toby's favorite, favorite, favorite game was finding things. She had such a good nose. She was always sniffing and exploring. And digging too! We would show her something like a shoe, a toy, or a cookie. Then we'd hide it and tell her to find it.

I can't remember hiding anything she didn't eventually find, even when we hid it inside something. She *always* found it. She had a great nose!

Even though she's gone, I like to imagine that Toby's little love spark is still as busy as ever, and we can still play the "find it" game. I tell her what I've lost and put her to work on it. I just go about my business until I get a hunch. Then I follow the hunch. I usually find whatever I've lost when I ask her to help.

So when I lost my glove, I asked Toby to help me find it. Then I stopped worrying about it and went about my business. I just waited for a hunch.

And my hunch was to look around here, even though I wasn't gardening around here yesterday.

Does it work?

As long as I imagine it will work, it seems to happen.

So you think up a play in your mind? Like we did yesterday?

Actually, it's even simpler than that. I think of Toby and call her name, just like I did when she was still here. And I trust her little spark will come running to find me. Then I talk to her, tell her my problem. And I ask her to show me where to find whatever it is that I can't find.

Then I wait until I get a hunch.

I pretty much talk to her the same way I did when she was here with me. We didn't stop being pals just because she died.

I haven't told anyone at school about how we imagine playing with Winnie. They'd think I'm nuts.

You think so? To me, talking to Toby is just another way of letting my mind play with possibilities. Just a different way than what we did to imagine playing with Winnie yesterday.

Maybe I've just imagined I can still talk to Toby's little spark so many times over the years that it just seems natural to me now.

Look! Over here! Behind the dogwood tree, up against the fence!

My glove! Thank you! Now I remember. I set the gloves down on top of the fence when I went out to get the garbage can. I must have picked one up and knocked the other off into the dog garden without noticing.

Thank you, Toby!

Why are you thanking her when she's dead?

Oh, saying thank you when you get help is always important. Gratitude feeds and waters the love sparks all around us. It makes them keep growing. It's very, very important to say thank you.

Could I ask Winnie to help me with things?

Certainly. Why not? Just call him and ask away.

Do you think he could help me find my homework?

Hmmm. That might be a little different. Is it really lost?

Sort of.

Right. So maybe you need to *do* your homework before you ask Winnie to help *find* the homework that's not even started? So it can't be lost yet? Getting help doesn't work THAT way!

But I think you already know that.

How did you know I haven't done it yet?

Well, since you just got off the bus and your books are still in your backpack, I figured your homework assignment was probably in there, too. But the homework wasn't likely to be finished yet.

Was that a hunch?

No, just good guessing.

Are you always a good guesser?

Sometimes. Not always! What is your homework today?

I have some math. That's easy for me. Then I'm supposed to write a story about flowers and draw a picture to go with it.

I can't think of what to write. It's such a lame assignment.

What about asking Winnie to help you with it?

Really?

Why not? You could beat your brains out trying to think up a topic. Or you could just wait for a hunch like I did with my glove. Or try closing your eyes and asking Winnie to help you see what to write about.

I know! I've got it!

Wow! That was fast.

Yeah! As soon as I closed my eyes, I saw our dog garden. I'll draw that! And tell about the dog flowers and their little jaws!

Sounds like a winner! Head home and get to work. I can't wait to see your picture story!

First, I'll get a snack. Then, I'll write about the dog garden! See you tomorrow!

CHAPTER 9

Love Cycles

Why the long face?

A girl on the bus said that the Rainbow Bridge was stupid and the Big Play was stupid, and I'm never going to see Winnie again. Ever. His spark burned out.

She was mean. So I told her she was ugly. U-G-L-Y. Ugly.

She did say some mean, hurtful things. And her kind of thinking steered the Big Play in a messy, not-so-good-feeling direction, so here you are feeling bad.

And that made you angry, and you wanted to make her feel bad too. So you called her ugly.

Yeah!

Did that make you feel any better?

I don't know about feeling better. But I got back at her!

Could we find a thought that might help steer you back toward feeling better?

What do you mean? How?

Well, thinking mean thoughts steers the Big Play in a mean direction. Thinking kind thoughts steers it in a kind direction. We can choose how we want to improvise in our play and imagine in our minds.

We can't change what *others* choose to think and say, but we can choose what *we* think and say.

I don't want to be nice to her.

Well, that's a choice. How does that make you feel?

Mean, like her, I guess.

Remember when we imagined different reasons why Winnie might have run out in the street? And it made you feel a little better to think of him as a hero?

Could you feel a little kinder toward the girl if you knew she was going home with a bad grade on a paper? And she knew her mom was going to be mad?

Or what if she just lost *her* dog and no one was helping her deal with feeling sad? So she took her feelings out on you?

I guess that would make me feel a little bit sorry for her. Maybe I would have just made a face at her instead of feeling mean and calling her ugly.

So, imagine something like that, something that helps you feel a little kinder, and put that thought into the Big Play.

I didn't really believe her about Winnie. I was just mad because she said it in front of all the other kids and tried to make me look stupid. I just wanted to get back at her.

I know.

Remember when I told you about the celebration we had for Winnie? After we planted the dog garden, there was something else we did.

From the look on your face, it was something serious.

It was. Kind of. We talked about getting another dog.

And you aren't sure about that?

I still keep wishing Winnie could come back. I still miss him. And if he's backstage in the Big Play, I don't want him to think I don't care about him anymore. I still love him. It would be fun to have a dog to play with again. But I don't want Winnie to be sad. Maybe he misses me as much as I miss him. I don't want him to think I'm forgetting him.

Is that true? Would you forget about Winnie if you had a new dog?

Well, I guess not really. But, like, Winnie was just always there for me. Always. No matter what I did. Or even when I wasn't so nice to him. At the playground, he always stayed with me. He never ran off with any other kids. He was so…

Loyal?

Yeah. Like that. I could always count on him, trust him. I feel like I'd be letting him down to get another dog. That makes me feel bad to think about getting another dog. But then I think it would be fun to have a dog again. And that makes me feel good.

I just don't know.

It's OK not to know what to do. Or to be unsure if what you're feeling is good or bad. Confusing, but perfectly normal. People's emotions often bounce around after losing a pet they've loved.

They do?

Sure. You know, love relationships like the one between you and Winnie run in cycles too. They're just like the cycles we talked about before. They're like plants coming up in spring, blooming into flowers, then going to seed and tucking themselves back into the ground again for the winter. Comings and goings. One cycle ends. Another begins. What seems to be an ending turns out to be a new beginning.

We just need to keep going and learn about life from how our dogs, cats, or other animals lived and died. To learn how to treat other people a little differently because of the way our pets loved us.

What do you mean, to keep going?

Well, it's normal to feel bad when you lose a dog. And it takes some time to deal with those mixed-up feelings. But if you keep on recycling your sad feelings over and over, you can get stuck there. You need to figure out a way to get unstuck and get going again with things that make you not sad, things you like to do that make you feel good.

Like when we can't get the Wi-Fi connection for our games, and my mom unplugs the box and then plugs it back in to start it again?

Something like that. Interesting example.

But how do people do that? Sometimes I feel better about losing Winnie, but then I feel sad again.

Well, it can be simple. But for a lot of people, it's hard.

Why?

Oh, lots of reasons. Sometimes feeling bad gets attention from other people. And if you like that attention, you might not want to stop those feelings.

Yeah. I get that. Since Winnie died, my mom's been letting us have a lot more cookies and ice cream instead of giving us peanut butter sandwiches and carrots after school!

I like cookies and ice cream too. I wouldn't want that to stop!

And I can see how thinking about getting another dog might make you feel a little better. But then you feel guilty about wanting another dog, and that makes you feel bad again.

Yeah, that's how I feel right now.

And so it goes. You bounce back and forth. We have the choice to cry or clap. But if you decide to reach for a little bit of a good feeling whenever a bad feeling drags you down, you eventually get yourself unstuck. You bounce one way, then the other, and back again. And as you keep working little by little to get unstuck, your heart starts to make a little room, and then a bit more space, and soon there can be enough room for a new dog to wiggle in.

I could never love another dog as much as Winnie.

Maybe. Maybe you'll never love another dog exactly the same way. But maybe you'll find you can love one just as much. Or even more. Letting go of the hurt doesn't mean you don't care about Winnie. And it doesn't mean you don't love him anymore. Or that he won't keep on loving you.

Remember, we're all in the Big Play. And we can choose our lines. Can you imagine the play a little bit? Instead of thinking, "What if Winnie was still here?" could you think, "What if I had a dog again that was just like Winnie?"

Tell me, was Winnie always perfect? Always good?

Well, no. Sometimes he took food off the kitchen counter when we weren't home. And he barked like crazy and knocked things over running to the door whenever the package man came. And…

And?

…if I left my sneakers out of the closet, he chewed the laces up. That made Mom really, really mad! At Winnie and at me! And if I didn't pay attention, he'd try to eat my ice cream when we went for cones. When he did that stuff, Mom used to say, "You little badness!"

Well, would you want another dog that did ALL those things all over again?

Maybe. But probably not.

So now you have a chance to imagine a dog with all the things you liked about Winnie but not any of his "badness."

What do you mean?

As you think about the kind of new dog that might be fun to have, you might say things like, "My new dog loves to fetch balls." "My new dog loves to sit and read with me." "My new dog loves to swim as much as I do." You might say, "I would like to have a dog with floppy ears." Pretty soon, you'd have a good list of things that would be nice to have in a new dog.

Kind of like a dog recipe!

Exactly! And that's another way the things you think about can steer the direction of the Big Play.

Think about backstage in the Big Play. The stagehands are listening. They hear your list of dog ingredients. They look around at all the dogs waiting to go on stage and find one with every single ingredient. And they get the dog's costume ready, and at just the right time, out he goes on stage and runs up to greet you.

So I can imagine the most amazing, best-ever dog in the world?

Whatever you want. But be prepared for surprises!

What do you mean?

Well, for one thing, maybe the stagehands will put the ingredients together in a way you hadn't thought about. You asked for floppy ears, but you forgot to mention legs. So your new dog has lovely, long, floppy ears, but he has short legs. So,his long, floppy ears drag on the ground, and they're always wet and muddy when he runs to give you a doggy kiss.

Or maybe you ask for a dog that loves to chase balls and get one that's the best chaser and catcher ever. But he runs away with the balls. He doesn't want to bring them back for you to throw again. And maybe your sister was thinking about a dog with certain ingredients, and your mom was thinking about a dog with certain ingredients.

When the stagehands find a dog with ALL those ingredients, your mom, your sister, and you might ALL be surprised! Be careful what you wish for, they say. Remember, we're all improvising together.

Hmmm, can I suggest an ingredient too? How about a quiet dog that doesn't bark and wake up Sammy too early in the morning!

Sure! But what will happen to Winnie if we get a new dog? Will his spark go out? Maybe the girl on the bus was right. Maybe he'd be gone forever.

No, Winnie's spark is love, and love never dies. Love is what the Big Play is all about. Winnie loved you, even when you scolded him. Or when you did something the grown-ups might have thought of as "badness," Winnie still loved you. And you loved him even when he chewed up a shoe, snatched your ice cream, or did some other kind of doggy mischief.

You learned about love from each other.

Can you still imagine Winnie standing backstage behind the curtain in the Big Play? Can you imagine him out of sight but still wiggling and wagging when he sees you, still loving you and encouraging you to be the best you can be as you play your part? Every time you remember him, you keep that love spark alive. And Winnie sends love right back to you. Love keeps us connected.

He was a great dog. I still miss him. But I guess I could talk to my mom, and dad, and sister about dog ingredients. That might be fun to think about.

There's something else that might be fun to think about. All that talk about ice cream made me want some. Run home and ask your mom if I can treat you and your sister to after-school cones at Toto's.

Can we buy a cone for Winnie too?

Absolutely. What flavor do you imagine he would like?

He can have anything but chocolate. Chocolate isn't good for dogs. But we're being silly, aren't we? How would he eat the cone?

Oh, I imagine we can find a way to make an extra cone disappear without a problem.

Epilogue

Sammy! Sammy! Hush. Hush. I know you love seeing Doogie, but you don't need to broadcast it to the whole neighborhood!

You'd better hang onto that leash before Doogie jumps the fence into my yard to join his girlfriend here!

That's funny! Do you think Doogie and Sammy are boyfriend-girlfriend?

Well, maybe not exactly in the way you might have a crush on someone at school. But dogs do like the company of other dogs, and these two seem to have hit it off pretty well ever since you and your sister started walking him for Mrs. Gordon. How about I get Sammy's leash and we take them for a walk together?

Sure! And, anyway, about Doogie...there's something I wanted to talk to you about.

Oh? Give me a minute to grab the leash and close up the house.

OK. Ready to go. So what's on your mind?

Mrs. Gordon is going to sell her house.

I heard about that when I got back from my vacation. When I visited her in the hospital after she had that stroke, she still couldn't talk very well, move one arm, or even get out of bed. She was home and doing OK before I left to visit my family. But I wondered if she could stay there, even with help.

Her son Jack asked my sister and me to walk Doogie every day for her. He wanted to pay us, but Mom wouldn't let him at first. She said it was just a neighborly thing to do, to help them with Doogie. But Jack insisted, and she gave in.

Know what we did?

Tell me!

We started a puppy fund to get a new dog! We're putting all the walking money in it.

What did your mom and dad say about that?

Dad's been all for getting another dog. But Mom says she isn't quite ready to deal with a new puppy. Mom says it's a lot of work and a lot of time to housetrain a puppy. And it wouldn't be fair to leave a puppy for a long time on the days she's at work and we're in school.

Puppy training can take time, for sure. I thought we'd never get our little Toby terrier potty-trained. But, by and by, she figured out that potty business was an outside job, not an inside one.

But GUESS what?

No idea! Tell me.

Well, yesterday, Jack asked us if we would like to have Doogie for our very own dog.

Really!

He stops to see Mrs. Gordon every day on his way home from work. When I went to walk Doogie, he said that the doctor doesn't think she'll be able to stay at home alone anymore.

She said something along those lines when I visited her Monday. So how do you feel about Jack's offer? If she can't stay at the house, I know she'll be worried about what will happen to Doogie.

Mrs. Gordon wants to live at that retirement place over on Grant Street. It's closer to Jack's house when she wants to go there. And Jack said they have a big garden and the apartments have kitchens. So she can still keep doing the baking and gardening she likes to do. There are lots of people there to help her if she needs help. But she can't keep Doogie there.

Anyway, Jack said we could have Doogie on one condition.

What's that?

He asked us to walk Doogie over to visit her once a week.

How do you kids feel about that?

Well, it's not too far to walk from here. And there are stoplights on the big crossings. Mom and Dad said it's up to my sister and me.

Sounds like you're not entirely sure about it, though.

Maybe. It's not about walking him over for visits. And we like Doogie. He's a neat dog. It's just that my sister and I have been thinking about puppies.

We've talked about what kind of dogs we like. I like Labs, but Mom and Dad think we should get a smaller dog. My sister likes Yorkies, but Dad thinks they might not be up to all the hiking and outdoor stuff we like to do.

Then, when Jack said we could have Doogie and we talked about taking him, Mom got out the dog recipe. Remember when I told you we made one?

I remember when you said that, but you never told me exactly what ingredients you put in it.

That's the thing. Doogie has just about all the ingredients we put in the recipe. Except he's not a puppy, and we don't know if he can swim. We want a dog that can swim with us like Winnie did.

That's interesting.

Yeah. But THAT's the thing! Mom noticed that we never wrote "puppy" as an ingredient, even though that's what my sister and I were thinking. We just wrote down "Things We Want in a Dog" at the top of the list. We never actually said "puppy," just "dog."

Well, that IS interesting!

We really like Doogie, but it would be fun to have a puppy.

We told Jack and Mrs. Gordon we'd let them know this weekend.

What will happen to Doogie if you don't take him?

Jack said he'd try to find another family to take him. His son is real allergic to dogs and gets hives and all sneezy around Doogie, even if he takes an allergy pill first. So they don't think it would work for them to take him.

But Mrs. Gordon wants Doogie to have a nice home, a special home, Jack said, where she would know that Doogie feels loved like she loves him.

So, on the one hand, a puppy means a lot of time and work to house-break and train. And on the other hand, there's Doogie, already housetrained. And a puppy would be more playful and fun than a grown dog like Doogie?

Not exactly. Doogie likes to play too. He's great at fetching! That's how Mrs. Gordon exercises him. But I thought it would be fun to train a dog myself and teach it tricks.

Does Doogie already know everything a dog can learn? Can he jump through your sister's hula-hoop? Can he find things you hide? Can he roll over? If he doesn't know how to swim, could *you* teach him?

He does some things. Like sit and stay and fetch. But not everything. Not those other things you said. I guess I could teach him new things, huh?

Like he was a puppy? He's pretty smart. He already knows all of our walking routes, and when we're heading home, he goes out in front and shows me the way. I don't even have to tell him when to make a turn!

In my experience, the fun of teaching a dog new things can go on as long as you have the interest and patience to do it. Doogie is still a young dog. And he sure seems to like you kids.

Yeah, he does. Mom said we'll talk again about taking him or not at dinner tonight. We can vote about it, and everyone's vote counts.

How do you think that might go?

Well, Mom and Dad will probably vote for taking him. I'm not sure about my sister. And after talking about it, I think I'll vote...

Doogie! Leave Sammy alone! They're so funny together. It looks like he's trying to kiss her.

The way they behave, I have to agree. If you gave her a say in whether or not Doogie moves in next door, I think Sammy would bark a loud, "Yes!"

Let's head back to my house and see if we can find any cookies.

Dog cookies or people cookies? Doogie and I BOTH love cookies!

I have a hunch we can find something for all our neighbors when we get back home.

What do you think, Sammy?

The End

Acknowledgments

No one ever writes a book alone. Looking back over this book's creation and revision, I count so many people whose encouragement and support moved it along. It is remarkable that a single kind word, spoken at the right time, can make such a difference in the outcome. I owe thanks to many more than are mentioned here.

My husband Bob gave me the means and space for this book to happen. Our sons Charlie and Paul and their families provided a supportive sounding board. My sisters Carol O'Shea and Sue Squiller listened and encouraged. My cousin Betty Haney's suggested readings pointed in interesting directions.

As the book took form, comments from early readers improved it. I appreciate the time and willingness to offer advice and critiques by Gail Bernson, Carolyn Cary, Jeanette Ciciora, Lyn Conway, Phillis Das, Debbie Devenny, Raffaello Di Meglio, Linnea Ehri, Victoria Hadden, Lisa Jacoby, Paul Kreitler, Erin Sherer, Antionette Martignoni, Rev. Dr. Richard McCaughey, Carol O'Shea, Debbie Rick Selski, Dr. Kathleen Smiler, Vivian Sorvall, and Sue Squiller.

Carole Ohl's magical Zentangle®-style illustrations portray dogs that once played among us. I want to thank Harper and Dan Braine, Phyllis and Pranab Das, Erin Sherer and Paul Kreitler, Ariane Mermod, Dr. Kathleen Smiler, Vivian Sorvall, and Sue Squiller for sharing their dog photos and stories.

The support of my meditation group kept me going as I struggled with new ways of understanding life's events and writing in a new (to me) genre. I thank them for offering the kind of nonjudgmental comradery we enjoy with our pets.

Grateful thanks to gentle Remy, the dog who was always close by as the book moved from a vague concept into manuscript form. Curled up near my computer, she kept me company through every keystroke. She went behind the curtain just before the words transitioned into book form. Her timing called me to walk my talk.

My deepest gratitude to Raffaello De Meglio and to Dick and Meredith McCaughy, who, by providing perspectives that made grief a bit more bearable after a family tragedy, planted the seeds from which this book grew.

About the Author

Photo credit: Kara Flannery

Family lore holds that Bonnie Kreitler's deep connection to animals began before she started talking. She combined journalism and animal science studies in college to turn her animal addiction into a career. Bonnie worked as a journalist and marketing consultant in the horse industry before starting Rambling Dog Publications. Her book *50 Careers with Horses!* was a best-seller in its niche. Learning to meditate led to studies of intuitive techniques and energy healing, including reiki and animal communication. She now writes for humans seeking deeper relationships with the animals in their lives. *When Winnie Went Away* is her first work of fiction. She lives in Connecticut.

About the Illustrator

Photo credit: Carole Ohl

Graphic designer and bead artist Carole Ohl became a certified Zentangle® teacher after a beading friend bugged her to check out the drawing technique online. Her dog illustrations are based on photos of real-life dogs. Carole lives physically in Ohio and online at openseed. etsy.com. Zentangle® is a registered trademark of Zentangle, Inc.

Disclaimer

This book is fiction. Any resemblance to persons or animals, living or dead, is purely coincidental.

The author hopes that anyone grieving the loss of a pet finds a bit of comfort from reading this book. She claims no professional counseling credentials.

This book is not a substitute for professional help for those struggling with grief. Any actions taken or not taken because of reading this book are the reader's sole responsibility.